James Gowdy Clark

Poetry and Song

James Gowdy Clark

Poetry and Song

ISBN/EAN: 9783744766982

Printed in Europe, USA, Canada, Australia, Japan

Cover: Foto ©Andreas Hilbeck / pixelio.de

More available books at **www.hansebooks.com**

James G. Clark

POETRY AND SONG.

BY

JAMES GOWDY CLARK.

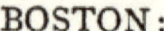

BOSTON:

D. LOTHROP AND COMPANY.

FRANKLIN AND HAWLEY STREETS.

To

My Daughter,

JENNIE CLARK JACOBSON,

ST. PAUL, MINN.

PREFACE.

THESE rhymes have been developed at intervals, and thrown off at random, during the past thirty-five years of a somewhat busy public life, involving almost constant travel, unaccompanied, until within the present year, by any serious view to their ultimate collection in a volume by themselves.

With the exception of the last poem in the book, — which is my latest production, and in which I attempt to give voice to the universal and " Divine Energy" that acts in unison with the Supreme Mind, — they are, as a rule, arranged without regard to the order in which they were first written.

A number of them are already familiar to the public through repeated appearance in the newspapers; and, with others less familiar, are now for the first time organized into a separate literary colony at the earnest request, not only of old and valued friends, but of strangers in all parts of the land.

No less than forty of the lyrics have been wedded to the author's own music, and to the music of other com-

posers, and issued in sheet form; and a few of these —
written long ago — treat of themes that, perhaps, would
not have been chosen later on in life, while others are
by no means up to the author's present standard of expression. But even these have friends who have sung,
or heard them sung, in times past, and who would miss
them, and be dissatisfied, were their favorites to be
excluded from the collection.

JAMES G. CLARK.

Minneapolis, Minn., June, 1886.

CONTENTS.

Contents.

SONGS AND BALLADS FOR MUSIC.

SPIRITUAL LYRICS.

LOVE SONGS AND POEMS.

MISCELLANEOUS.

POETRY AND SONG.

THE VOICE OF THE PEOPLE.

Swing inward, O gates of the future!
  Swing outward, ye doors of the past,
For the soul of the people is moving
  And rising from slumber at last;
The black forms of night are retreating,
  The white peaks have signalled the day,
And Freedom her long roll is beating,
  And calling her sons to the fray.

And woe to the rule that has plundered
  And trod down the wounded and slain,
While the wars of the Old Time have thundered,
  And men poured their life-tide in vain;
The day of its triumph is ending,
  The evening draws near with its doom,
And the star of its strength is descending,
  To sleep in dishonor and gloom.

Though the tall trees are crowned on the highlands
  With the first gold of rainbow and sun,

While far in the distance below them
   The rivers in dark shadows run,
They must fall, and the workmen shall burn them
   Where the lands and the low waters meet,
And the steeds of the New Time shall spurn them
   With the soles of their swift-flying feet.

Swing inward, O gates! till the morning
   Shall paint the brown mountains in gold,
Till the life and the love of the New Time
   Shall conquer the hate of the Old;
Let the face and the hand of the Master
   No longer be hidden from view,
Nor the lands he prepared for the many
   Be trampled and robbed by the few.

The soil tells the same fruitful story,
   The seasons their bounties display,
And the flowers lift their faces in glory
   To catch the warm kisses of day;
While our fellows are treated as cattle
   That are muzzled when treading the corn,
And millions sink down in Life's battle
   With a sigh for the day they were born.

Must the Sea plead in vain that the River
   May return to its mother for rest,
And the Earth beg the rain clouds to give her
   Of dews they have drawn from her breast?

The Voice of the People.

Lo! the answer comes back in a mutter
   From domes where the quick lightnings glow,
And from heights where the mad waters utter
   Their warning to dwellers below.

And woe to the robbers who gather
   In fields where they never have sown,
Who have stolen the jewels from labor
   And builded to Mammon a throne;
For the snow-king, asleep by the fountains,
   Shall wake in the summer's hot breath,
And descend in his rage from the mountains,
   Bearing terror, destruction, and death.

And the throne of their god shall be crumbled,
   And the sceptre be swept from his hand,
And the heart of the haughty be humbled,
   And a servant be chief in the land, —
And the Truth and the Power united
   Shall rise from the graves of the True,
And the wrongs of the Old Time be righted
   In the might and the light of the New.

For the Lord of the harvest hath said it,
   Whose lips never uttered a lie,
And his prophets and poets have read it
   In symbols of earth and of sky:
That to him who has revelled in plunder
   Till the angel of conscience is dumb,

The shock of the earthquake and thunder
   And tempest and torrent shall come.

Swing inward, O gates of the future !
   Swing outward, ye doors of the past,
A giant is waking from slumber
   And rending his fetters at last ;
From the dust where his proud tyrants found him,
   Unhonored and scorned and betrayed,
He shall rise with the sunlight around him,
   And rule in the realm he has made.

THE MOUNT OF THE HOLY CROSS.

The "Mount of the Holy Cross," the principal mountain of the Saguache Range, Colorado, is 14,176 feet above tide-water. The Cross is located near the top, facing the east, and consists of two crevices filled with snow summer and winter. The crevices are about fifty feet wide, and the snow in them from fifty to one hundred feet in depth. The perpendicular arm of the Cross is some fifteen hundred feet long, and the horizontal arm seven hundred feet. The Cross can be seen at a distance of thirty or forty miles.

THE ocean divided, the land struggled through,
And a newly born continent burst into view;
Like furrows upturned by the ploughshare of God,
The mountain chains rose where the billows had
    trod;
And their towering summits, in mighty array,
Turned their terrible brows to the glare of the day,
Like sentinels guarding the gateway of Time,
Lest the contact with mortals should stain it with
    crime.

The ocean was vanquished, the new world was born.
Its headlands flung back the bold challenge of morn;
The sun from the trembling sea marshalled the mist
Till the hills by the soul of the ocean were kissed;
And the Winter-king reached from his cloud-castled
    height
To hang on each brow the first garland of white;

For the crystals came forth at the touch of his wand,
And the soul of the sea ruled again on the land.

Then arose the loud moan of the desolate tide,
As it called back its own from the far mountain side:
" O soul of my soul! by the sun led astray,
Return to the heart that would hold thee alway;
The sun and the silver moon woo me in vain,
By day and by night I am sobbing with pain;
Oh, loved of my bosom! Oh, child of the Free,
Come back to the lips that are waiting for thee!"

But a sound, like all melodies mingled in one,
Came down through the spaces that cradled the
    sun.
Like music from far-distant planets it fell,
Till earth, air, and ocean were hushed in the spell:
" Be silent, ye waters, and cease your alarm,
All motion is only the pulse of my arm;
In my breath the vast systems unerringly swing,
And mine is the chorus the morning stars sing.

" 'Twas mine to create them, 'tis mine to command
The land to the ocean, the sea to the land;
All, all are my creatures, and they who would give
True worship to me for each other must live.
Lo! I leave on the mountain a sign that shall be
A type of the union of land and sea, —
An emblem of anguish that comes before bliss,
For they who would conquer must conquer by this."

The roar of the earthquake in answer was heard,
The land from its solid foundation was stirred,
The breast of the mountain was rent by the shock,
And a cross was revealed on the heart of the rock;
One hand pointing south, where the tropic gales
    blow,
And one to the kingdom of winter and snow,
While its face turned to welcome the dawn from afar,
Ere Jordan had rolled under Bethlehem's star.

The harp of the elements over it swung,
In the wild chimes of Nature its advent was rung,
Around it the hair of the Winter-king curled,
Against it in fury his lances were hurled,
And the pulse of the hurricane beat in its face
Till the snows were locked deep in its mighty em-
    brace,
And its arms were outstretched on the mountain's
    cold breast,
As spotless and white as the robes of the blest.

Then the spirit of Summer came up from the south
With the smile of the Junes on her beautiful mouth,
And breathed on the valleys, the plains, and the
    hills,
While the snow rippled home in the arms of the
    rills;
The winter was gone, but the symbol was there,
Towering mutely and grand, like the angel of prayer,

Where the morning shall stream on the place of its
    birth
Till the last cross is borne by the toilers of earth.

It will never grow old while the sea-breath is drawn
From the lips of the billows at evening and dawn,
While heaven's pure finger transfigures the dews,
And with garlands of frost-work its beauty renews;
It was there when the blocks of the pyramid pile
Were drifting in sands on the plains of the Nile,
And it still shall point homeward, a token of trust,
When pyramids crumble in dimness and dust.

It shall lean o'er the world like a banner of peace
Till discord and war between brothers shall cease,
Till the red sea of Time shall be cleansed of its gore,
And the years like white pebbles be washed to the
    shore;
As long as the incense from ocean shall rise
To weave its bright woof on the warp of the skies,
As long as the clouds into crystals shall part,
That cross shall gleam high on the Continent's heart.

NOVEMBER.

THE red sun gathers up his beams,
  To bid the withered earth farewell,
And voices from the swelling streams
  Are mingling with the evening bell;
The cold lake sobs with restless grief,
  Where late the water-lilies grew,
While autumn fowl, and autumn leaf,
  Are sailing down the rivers blue.

Forsaken are the woodland shrines,
  The bluebird and the wren have fled,
And winds are wailing through the pines
  A dirge for summer's glorious dead;
E'en man forsakes his daily strife,
  And muses on the bright things flown,
As if in Nature's changing life
  He saw the picture of his own.

I often think, at this sad hour,
  As evening weeps her earliest tear,
And sunset gilds the naked bower,
  And waves are breaking cold and clear,

Of that glad time, whose memory dwells
  Like starlight o'er life's cloudy weather,
When side by side we roved the dells
  Of dear New England's coast together.

'Twas on old Plymouth's rock-famed shore,
  One calm November night with thee,
I watched the long light trembling o'er
  The billows of the eastern sea;
The weary day had sunk to rest
  Beyond the lines of leafless wood,
And guardian clouds, from south to west,
  Arrayed in hues of crimson stood.

We climbed the hill of noble graves,
  Where the stern patriarchs of the land
Seemed listening to the same grand waves
  That freed them from the oppressor's hand;
We talked of spirits pure and kind,
  With gentle forms and loving eyes, —
Of happy homes we left behind,
  In vales beneath the western skies.

A few brief days, — and when the earth
  Grew white around the traveller's feet,
And bright fires blazed on every hearth,
  We parted never more to meet
Until I go where thou art gone,
  From this dark world of death and blight,
And walk with thee above the sun
  That sank upon thy grave to-night.

I hear the muffled tramp of years
   Come stealing up the slope of Time;
They bear a train of smiles and tears,
   Of burning hopes and dreams sublime:
But future years may never fling
   A treasure from their passing hours,
Like those that come on sleepless wing,
   From memory's golden plain of flowers.

The morning breeze of long ago
   Sweeps o'er my brain with soft control,
Fanning the embers to a glow
   Amidst the ashes round my soul;
And by the dim and flickering light
   I see thy beauteous form appear,
Like one returned from wanderings bright,
   To bless my lonely moments here.

MY MOTHER IS NEAR.

SWEET mother, the birds from our bowers have fled,
  The reaper has gathered his sheaves,
The glorious summer lies silent and dead,
  And the land like a pale mourner grieves;
But the garden of mem'ry is blooming to-day
  With flowers and leaves ever new,
And the birds and the fountains around it that play
  Are singing, dear mother, of you.

Like green shores receding beyond the blue seas
  Seem the years by your tenderness blest,
And youth's merry music grows faint on the breeze
  That is wafting me on to life's west;
Yet beautiful seems the mild glance of your eye,
  And the blessing your fond spirit gave,
As the mists of the valley hang bright in the sky
  Though the mountains are lost in the wave.

I wonder, sometimes, if the souls that have flown
  Return to the mourners again,
And I ask for a sign from the trackless unknown
  Where millions have questioned in vain;

I see not your meek, loving face through the strife
  That would blind me with doubting and fear,
But a voice murmurs " Peace " to the tumult of life,
  And I know that my mother is near.

The cold world may cover my pathway with frowns,
  And mingle with bitter each joy;
It may load me with crosses, and rob me of crowns,
  I have treasures it cannot destroy:
There's a green, sunny isle in the depths of my soul
  Whose roses the winds never strew,
And the billows and breezes around it that roll
  Bring tidings of heaven and you.

THE CAPTAIN'S SIGNAL.

I AM safe in port, but I watch and wait
For another boat to bring my Mate, —
The faithful Mate, who, in calm and strife,
Had cruised with me o'er the seas of life.
I left our crew at the close of day, —
It is hardly a cable's length away, —
And stepped ashore in a quiet bay;
A silver cloud on the lowlands lay,
And through the mist, by a radiant band,
I was borne across o'er the border land.

And my Mate sits gazing out through tears,
For her heart goes back to our youthful years,
When all the storms of the ocean wide
Might beat and break o'er the good ship's side,
And never a sturdy spar or mast
Would yield at the rage of tide or blast,
And never a sail at the storm-king's frown,
Like a frightened bird would flutter down,
And never a spar nor a timber start
From her maintop high to her oaken heart.

O Mate of my life! though hid from view
By the silver mist, I am guarding you,
And will linger near till the day is done,
And the white sail furled in the western sun;
When the boat-keel grates on the golden strand,
Ere the hulk sinks down in the shifting sand,
I will welcome you to the bright green land, —
You shall see my face, you will grasp my hand,
And wander with me the New Realm o'er,
Where the dreams of youth can be lost no more.

OCEAN MUSINGS. .

The sun has hid his fiery eye
'Neath quiet evening's jewelled brow,
And from her yellow casement in the sky
The musing moon is gazing now:
The clear, soft glimmer of her crown
Behind us paves the waters wide,
While, from their distant walls, her guards look down
To see their faces in the tide.

A spell of tranquil glory binds
The bosom of the voiceless deep,
And, gently dimpled by the powerless winds,
The waves in laughing beauty sleep:
And, basking 'neath the dreamy smiles
Of mingled shade and misty light,
Lie the dim summits of our native isles,
Reposing in the arms of night.

Slowly our bark, to realms more new,
Moves on before the moving moon,
While we look back to take our lingering view,
Through night's mysterious summer noon,

Of happy scenes forever flown, —
Scenes which now beam from yon loved shore,
More bright than when we deemed them all our own,
And time flew lightly, gayly o'er.

Thus, when the sun of Hope's bright day
Sinks down behind Life's lonely main,
Will the mild moon of memory lend her ray,
Disclosing those fair scenes again,
Where sleep the smiles of youth's lost dream:
And manhood's eye with tears shall fill,
To see the waves of vanished glory gleam
More lovely and enchanting still.

THE SILVER PILGRIM.

WE knew him many years ago,
One of a band of noble boys,
On old Chautauqua's grassy plains,
A stranger to life's bitter pains,
Before his deep **eyes** caught the glow
Of manhood's **graver aims and** joys:
Before ambition's fever dream
Had launched him on the restless stream
Of human lives, that surged and rolled
Across the world **in search of** gold, —
The stream **whose bed is** filled with graves
Of thousands strangled in the waves
While looking out with eager eyes
Toward the ever-flitting prize, —
The stream whose noisy billows **chase**
Around the Rocky Mountains' base,
Then rolling on, with tumult fills
The silver city of the hills,[1]
Whence leap the ocean's new-born rills,
The mountain **city of the** West, —
A hammock swung from crest to **crest,**
A hammock hung to fast'nings **rude**
Up in the awful solitude

[1] Leadville, Colorado.

Where twice ten thousand souls abide
Ten thousand feet above the tide
That kisses with its foamy lips
The keels of fifty thousand ships,
And clutches with its briny hands
The outlines of a thousand lands.

The years rolled by, — his feet had pressed
    The trails that cross the high divide
That sends its fountains east and west,
    To inland sea and ocean wide ;
And still the same unrest remained
    That chafes in every earnest soul
Which strives for objects unattained,
    Yet knows that earth holds not the goal.

And when, at last, "his time had come,"
    Before the years that mark man's prime
Had fallen from the boughs of time,
    It found him where the busy hum
Of stranger voices rose and fell,
While yet a parent's late farewell,
From hearts that were too full to speak,
Was lingering fresh on lip and cheek.

On one of those soft summer's days
    Which only mountain regions know,
Where earth is like a hymn of praise,
    And heaven seems list'ning near and low,
They brought him to the " miner's rest,"
With fever in his weary breast,

But in his soul that holy trust
Which comes at last to cheer the just.

There knelt beside that sacred bed
   But two from all the household band,
And when the last low words were said,
   A sister's lips, a brother's hand,
Were softly laid on cheek and head,
   As if to waft across the land,
O'er mountains vast and deserts drear,
The signs which all would wish to hear.

The August moon was fair and young,
Its crescent o'er Mt. Massive hung,
And touched with silver-tinted lines
The solemn canyons, rocks, and pines;
And midnight stars look softly down
Upon the Mammon-haunted town,
As though they viewed with mournful ken
The griefs that cloud the homes of men.

Without a struggle or a sigh,
To hint that death was passing by,
He joined the angels from the sky,
And calmly crossed the border-line
   Beyond life's crest of rock and snow,
And saw the hills immortal shine,
   And heard the fountain's heavenward flow,
Where peace shall crown the weary heart
   With sweeter rest than mortals find,
And never from the eye shall start
   The tears that prove the troubled mind.

THE WOOD ROBIN.

How calmly the lingering light
  Beams back over woodland and plain,
As an infant, ere closing its eyelids at night,
  Looks back on its mother again.

The wood robin sings at my door,
  And her song is the sweetest I hear
From all the sweet birds that incessantly pour
  Their notes through the noon of the year.

'Twas thus in my boyhood time,
  That season of emerald and gold,
Ere the storms and the shadows that fall on our
      prime
  Had told me that pleasures grow old;

I loved, in the warm summer eves,
  To recline on the welcoming sod,
By the broad spreading temple of twilight and
      leaves,   .
  Where the wood robin worshipped her God.

I knew not that life could endure
    The burden it beareth to-day,
And I felt that my soul was as happy and pure
    As the tones of the wood robin's lay.

Oh beautiful, beautiful youth,
    With its visions of hope and love,
How cruel is life to reveal us the truth,
    That peace only liveth above !

The wood robin trills the same tune
    From her thicket in garden and glen ;
And the landscape and sky, and the twilight of
        June,
    Look lovely and glowing as then. —

But I think of the glories that fell
    In the harvest of sorrow and tears,
Till the song of the forest bird sounds like a knell,
    Tolling back through the valley of years.

Sweet bird, as thou singest, forlorn
    Though the visions that rise from the past,
The deep of the future is purpling with morn,
    And its mystery melting at last.

I know that the splendor of youth
    Will return to me yet, and my soul
Will float in the sunlight of beauty and truth,
    Where the tides of the Infinite roll.

Oh! I fain would arise and set sail
  From the lowlands of trouble and pain;
But I wait on the shore for the tarrying gale,
  And sigh for the haven in vain.

And I watch for the ripples to play
  And tell me the breezes are nigh,
Like a sailor who longs to be wafted away
  To the lands that lie hid in the sky.

But the whippoorwill wails on the moor,
  And day has deserted the west;
The moon glimmers down through the vines at my
      door,
  And the robin has flown to her nest.

Adieu, gentle bird! Ere the sun
  Shall line the green forest with light,
Thou'lt wake from thy slumber more merry than one
  Who heard thee and blest thee to-night.

OUTCAST.

ALAS for her who sits alone
   Beside the sepulchre of hope,
With none to roll away the stone
   And bid the flowers that lined life's slope
Return once more, and fill the gloom
With sweeter life and fresher bloom :
Better for her the voiceless tomb,
Without a sign to mark the spot
Except the blue forget-me-not,
That sits upon the lap of spring
Before the robins come to sing,
   Or bluebirds pipe their flute-like tunes ;
Before the icy chains are riven
   That fetter fountain, lake, and river,
And from the snows that chill the sod
Looks up to greet the eye of God,
   A promise of celestial Junes,
When in the quickening light of Heaven
   Our dead shall live and bloom forever.

BY THE BORDERS OF THE SEA.

By the borders of the sea,
   On his couch the Ruler lay,
With death's twilight slowly creeping
   Through the noontide of his day;
And the waves' complaining moan,
   And the breathing of the spray,
      Drifted upward from the bosom
      Of the bay.

From that window looking out
   O'er the ocean's ebb and flow,
How his weary heart goes backward
   To the land of long ago,
Where a little cabin stands,
   While the trees wave to and fro,
      And his mother's voice is singing
      Sweet and low.

And that mother prays alone
   When the toil of day is done,
That the struggling boy may conquer
   In life's battle just begun;

But she dreams not of a time
   When, with shouts of victory won,
     All the nation shall be turning
       To her son.

  From that quiet cabin home
    To the marble halls of state
Is a life-track winding upward,
  'Neath the golden star of fate;
At the end a sorrowing race
  With bowed hearts in silence wait,
    While immortal hands swing open
      Glory's gate.

SWEET RUTH.

THE summer will soon be here, sweet Ruth;
   For the birds of brighter bowers
Are singing their way from the balmy south
   To the land of opening flowers.
But the summer will fade, and the flowers will die,
   And the birds from bank and plain
Go mourning back to a warmer sky,
   While I wait for thee in vain.

Oh! many a heart and many a hand,
   I have prized in pain and bliss,
Have found that rest in a better land
   Which they never knew in this;
And of all the forms that have fled with thee,
   From a kingdom fraught with tears,
There are none that seem like thine to me
   Through the golden mist of years.

But I never have wished thee back, sweet Ruth,
   In the years that since have rolled;
And I guard the memory of thy truth
   As a miser would his gold:

The loneliest glens of my being know
  How the birds of peace may sing,
And the darkest waves have caught the glow
  From a guardian angel's wing.

TO DR. JAMES C. JACKSON.

GRAND Prophet of Life, when thy sun shall go down,
And clouds fade in glory that gathered in frown,
And the lives thou hast blessed with thine own life
    and light
Shine forth like the stars in the dome of the night,
Thou shalt look o'er the labor-worn track of the
    past,
And thy spirit rejoice in its travail at last;
The crown of the victor shall rest on thy brow,
And mortals behold thee as angels do now.

ART THOU LIVING YET?

Is there no grand, immortal sphere
    Beyond this realm of broken ties,
To fill the wants that mock us here,
    And dry the tears from weeping eyes?
Where Winter melts in endless Spring,
    And June stands near with deathless flowers,
Where we may hear the dear ones sing
    Who loved us in this world of ours?
I ask, and lo ! my cheeks are wet
    With tears for one I cannot see :
O mother, art thou living yet,
    And dost thou still remember me ?

I feel thy kisses o'er me thrill,
    Thou unseen angel of my life ;
I hear thy hymns around me trill
    An undertone to care and strife ;
Thy tender eyes upon me shine,
    As from a being glorified,
Till I am thine and thou art mine,
    And I forget that thou hast died :
I almost lose each vain regret
    In visions of a life to be :

But, mother, art thou living yet,
  And dost thou still remember me?

The Springtimes bloom, the Summers fade,
  The Winters blow along my way;
But over every light or shade
  Thy memory lives by night and day;
It soothes to sleep my wildest pain,
  Like some sweet song that cannot die,
And, like the murmur of the main,
  Grows deeper when the storm is nigh:
I know the brightest stars that set
  Return to bless the yearning sea, —
But, mother, art thou living yet,
  And dost thou still remember me?

I sometimes think thy soul comes back
  From o'er the dark and silent stream,
Where last we watched thy shining track,
  To those green hills of which we dream;
Thy loving arms around me twine,
  My cheeks bloom younger in thy breath,
Till thou art mine and I am thine,
  Without a thought of pain or death:
And yet, at times my eyes are wet
  With tears for her I cannot see:
O mother, art thou living yet,
  And dost thou still remember me?

THE BIRD OF WASHINGTON.

WHEN the winds are unchained o'er the plains of the
        world,
    And clouds burst their bonds on the hills,
When the banner of storm o'er the deep is unfurled,
    And terror the human heart thrills, —
'Tis then that I fly to my aerie on high,
And gaze on the battle of billow and sky:
I laugh in my glee while the elements rave,
And they call me the bird of the Brave.

When Liberty looks on the woes of the world
    Through clouds of oppression and crime,
When tyrants and knaves from their high thrones
        are hurled,
    And men break the fetters of Time, —
'Tis then that I rise on the death-rolling night,
And strike for the brave in the battle of Right:
I laugh as the legions of tyranny flee,
And they call me the bird of the Free.

STAR OF THE NORTH.

STAR of Freedom burning high
In the cold, dark northern sky,
See the suff'rer turn to thee,
Guide him safe from slavery.

CHORUS.

Star of the North, we follow thee,
We follow thee to Liberty,
Nor dread the snows of Canada,
With freedom's blood to warm our veins,
And freedom's fire to melt our chains.

When our hearts, bowed low with toil,
Bleed upon a tyrant's soil,
Through the gloom of slavery's night,
Star of Freedom, pour thy light.

When the bloodhound's angry howl
Thrills with fear the faltering soul, —
When for life we struggling pray,
Star of Freedom, gild the way,

When we drop the galling chain,
When the promised land we gain,
When we dwell where men are free,
Still, bright star, we'll turn to thee.

A PROPHECY (*1852*).

How glorious, how grandly bright
  Above the dark and suffering Earth,
The Sun comes forth in deathless might!
  He has a smile for every hearth,
And shines alike on scenes of crime
  And paths of angel purity,
But never on a fairer clime
  Than that from which a slave must flee
To find the boon his spirit craves,
Yet cannot find where proudly waves
  The starry banner of the Free.
Children of Afric's burning skies,
  Columbia's eagle yet will rise,
And spread above your bleeding forms
  The pity of his sheltering wings, —
Wings that have braved the raging storms
  Which rock the thrones of despot kings!
For Hope looks from the clouds above,
  And Liberty's clear bells are ringing,
And generous hearts, like flowers of love,
  From every mountain-side are springing.
From California's yellow sands
  To old Niagara's mighty fall,

Where the broad lakes of Northern lands
   Leap madly from their mountain wall,
They come, — they come in robes of light,
   With Freedom's lightning blazing o'er them:
They're bursting through Oppression's night,
   And tyrants fly in dread before them.

FREMONT'S BATTLE HYMN.

OH, spirits of Washington, Warren, and Wayne !
Oh, shades of the heroes and patriots slain !
Come down from your mountains of emerald and
    gold,
And smile on the banner ye cherished of old ;
Descend in your glorified ranks to the strife,
Like legions sent forth from the armies of life ;
Let us feel your deep presence as waves feel the
    breeze,
When white fleets like snowflakes are drowned in
    the seas.

As the red lightnings run on the black, jagged cloud,
Ere the thunder-king speaks from his wind-woven
    shroud,
So gleams the bright steel along valley and shore,
Ere the conflict shall startle the land with its roar :
As the veil which conceals the clear starlight is
    riven
When clouds strike together, by warring winds
    driven,
So the blood of the race must be offered like rain,
Ere the stars of our country are ransomed again.

Proud sons of the soil where the palmetto grows,
Once patriots and brothers, now traitors and foes,
Ye have turned from the path which our forefathers
    trod,
And stolen from man the best gift of his God, —
Ye have trampled the tendrils of love in the
    ground,
Ye have scoffed at the laws which the Nazarene
    found,
Till the great wheel of justice seemed blocked for a
    time,
And the eyes of humanity blinded with crime.

The hounds of Oppression were howling the knell
Of martyrs and prophets at gibbet and cell,
While Mercy despaired of the blossoming years
When her harpstrings no more shall be rusted with
    tears ;
But God never ceases to strike for the right,
And the ring of His anvil came down through the
    night,
Though the world was asleep and the Nation seemed
    dead,
And Truth into bondage by Error was led.

Will the banners of morn at your bidding be furled,
When the day-king arises to quicken the world?
Can ye cool the fierce fires of his heat-throbbing
    breast,
Or turn him aside from his goal in the west?

Ah! sons of the plains where the orange-tree
    blooms,
Ye may come to our pine-covered mountains for
    tombs,
But the light ye would smother was kindled by One
Who gave to the universe planet and sun.

Go strangle the throat of Niagara's wrath,
Till he utters no sound on his torrent-cut path;
Go bind his great sinews of rock-wearing waves,
Till he begs at your feet like your own fettered
    slaves;
Go cover his pulses with sods from the ground,
Till he hides from your sight like a hare from the
    hound;
Then swarm to our borders, and silence the notes
That thunder of Freedom from millions of throats.

Come on with your chattels, all worn, from the soil
Where men receive scourging in payment for toil;
Come, robbers! come, traitors! we welcome you all,
As the leaves of the forest are welcomed by fall:
The birthright of manhood awaits for your slaves,
But prisons and halters are waiting for knaves;
And the blades of our freemen are longing to rust
With their blood who would bury our stars in the
    dust.

They fade unlamented from life and from sight
Whose lives are but shadows on Liberty's light;

They slumber unblest by fraternity's star
Who have blocked up the track of humanity's car;
Regarded, when dead, by the wise and the good,
As shepherds regard the dead wolf in the wood,
And only unhated when Heaven shall efface
The memory of wrong from the souls of the race.

The streams may forget how they mingled our gore,
And the myrtle entwine on their borders once more;
The song-birds of Peace shall return to our glades,
And children clasp hands where their fathers clashed
    blades;
Columbia shall rise from her trial of fire
More pure than she came from the hand of her sire:
But Freedom will point the cold finger of scorn
When History tells where her traitors were born

THE CHILDREN OF THE BATTLE-FIELD.

Upon the field of Gettysburg
   The summer sun was high,
When Freedom met her haughty foe
   Beneath a northern sky.
Among the heroes of the North
   That swelled her grand array,
And rushed like mountain eagles forth
   From happy homes away,
There stood a man of humble fame,—
   A sire of children three,—
And gazed within a little frame
   His pictured ones to see:
And blame him not if, in the strife,
   He breathed a soldier's prayer,—
"O Father! shield the soldier's wife,
   And for his children care."

Upon the field of Gettysburg,
   When morning shone again,
The crimson cloud of battle burst
   In streams of fiery rain:

Our legions quelled the awful flood
  Of shot and steel and shell,
While banners, marked with ball and blood,
  Around them rose and fell :
And none more nobly won the name
  Of champion of the Free
Than he who pressed the little frame
  That held his children three ;
And none were braver in the strife
  Than he who breathed the prayer, —
"O Father ! shield the soldier's wife,
  And for his children care."

Upon the field of Gettysburg
  The full moon slowly rose, —
She looked, and saw ten thousand brows
  All pale in death's repose ;
And down beside a silver stream,
  From other forms away,
Calm as a warrior in a dream,
  Our fallen comrade lay ;
His limbs were cold, his sightless eyes
  Were fixed upon the three
Sweet stars that rose in memory's skies
  To light him o'er death's sea.
Then honored be the soldier's life,
  And hallowed be his prayer, —
"O Father ! shield the soldier's wife,
  And for his children care."

MINNIE MINTON.

MINNIE MINTON, in the shadow
　　I have waited here alone, —
On the battle's gory meadow,
　　Which the scythe of death has mown,
I have listened for your coming
　　Till the dreary dawn of day,
But I only hear the drumming,
　　As the armies march away.

CHORUS.

O Minnie! dear Minnie,
　　I have heard the angel's warning,
I have seen the golden shore;
　　I will meet you in the morning
Where the shadows come no more, —
　　Nevermore, nevermore.

Minnie Minton, I am wounded,
　　And I know that I must die,
By a stranger host surrounded,
　　And no loved one kneeling nigh;
And I fain would hear you whisper
　　In the twilight cold and gray,

But I only hear the tramping
  As the armies march away.

Minnie Minton, I am weary,
  And I long to reach my goal;
Yet the billows of old Erie
  Blue upon my memory roll;
And I pause to hear you singing
  By the waters of the bay,
But I only hear the bugles
  As the armies march away.

Minnie Minton, I've been dreaming
  Of those moments gone before,
Ere I saw the sabres gleaming
  On the fields of death and gore;
And I thought that you were kneeling
  O'er the turf whereon I lay,
But I woke to see the banners
  As the armies march away.

Minnie Minton, I am dying.
  As the world recedes from view,
I can see the old flag flying
  O'er the rebel rag of blue;
I behold the heroes saintly
  Who have fallen in the fray,
And their bugles warble faintly
  As they beckon me away.

FREEDOM'S DEAD.

AH! green their glory long will be
Who give their lives to liberty;
Their names will linger broad and bright
When other names are lost to sight;
Their memory will dearer grow
While sounding seas and rivers flow;
And, though the world is black with crime,
Their fame shall live, a light sublime,
A pillar of deliverance burning,
To which th' oppressed, for Freedom yearning
May turn, as Israel turned of yore,
And view from far the Promised Shore.

SOUGHT BUT NEVER FOUND.

WE'LL sing to-night of other times
   That bloomed along the years
Ere war had clanged its iron chimes,
   And filled our homes with tears;
And we'll recall a gallant form
   That sleeps among the slain,
And dream that, safe from shot and storm,
   Our brother lives again.

We know the flag for which he died
   May never more be furled;
We know our land, though crucified,
   Will rise and bless the world, —
But hearts must bleed while lands rejoice,
   And States forget their strife:
We long to hear our brother's voice
   Blend with the sounds of life.

The God of Peace rolls back the gloom,
   And stills the combat's roar,
And bursting shell, and cannon's boom,
   Are heard in wrath no more;

But who may count their distant graves,
    Unmarked by name or mound,
Who, 'mid the home-returning braves,
    Were sought but never found?

WHEN YOU AND I WERE SOLDIER BOYS.

OH, the stormy times we knew,
In our suit of army blue,
When you and I were soldier boys together, Will;
Ere they laid you in the soil,
Where a glory crowns your toil
As the springtime crowns the gloomy winter weather,
Will.

CHORUS.

Oh, gallant, gallant Will,
Your noble heart is still
Where the river waves roll in the sun;
You never more will thrill
At the wild bugle's trill,
Nor wake at the roar of the gun, —
Nor march to the war drum rolling,
Nor march to the war drum rolling,
Nor march to the war drum rolling,
Nor shout when the battle is won.

Ah! we loved each other more
For the trials that we bore,

When you and I were soldier boys in battle, Will;
    And our hearts the stronger grew
    For the dangers we passed through,
'Mid cannons' crash and rifles' deadly rattle, Will.

          CHORUS.

    Though my fighting time has passed
    Like a storm upon the blast,
And I walk no more among the dead and dying,
    Will,
    I recall the days with pride
    When we battled side by side,
And the stripes and stars above our heads were
    flying, Will.

          CHORUS.

    And I still remember you,
    Of the many tried and true,
Who slumber now in southern glen and valley, Will;
    And sometimes in a dream
    Will the old flag o'er me stream,
While the spirits of the brave around it rally, Will.

          CHORUS.

SCOTLAND, I LOVE THEE.

O Scotland! I love thee: I cling to thee yet,
　As a young maiden clings to her lover;
I love thy gray mountains, and never forget
　The glens which their dark shadows cover;
I know that the long weary leagues of the main
　Now hide thy green valleys from me,
And I know that I never may tread them again, —
　Yet, Scotland, I'm dreaming of thee.

O Scotland, I love thee: I turn to thy shore
　With a song for each scene of my childhood,
As a bird o'er the billow where rough waters roar
　Will turn to her nest in the wildwood:
Then give me the storm-braving headlands that
　　stand
　Like sentinels guarding the sea,
The homes and the hearts of my dear native land, —
　O Scotland! I'm dreaming of thee.

AMERICA AND IRELAND.

WE will not forget thee, old Ireland, now
   That the storm-cloud hangs over thy borders,
And the sigh of submission expires in a vow
   To be free as thy girdle of waters :
The leaves of the shamrock are spreading afar,
   And we honor the heroes who bore them,
When Sheridan, Mulligan, Corchran, and Meagher
   Like pillars of fire went before them.

The roar of the lion is heard in the night,
   As he drinks from the depths of thy fountains ;
But the eagles are pluming their pinions for flight
   On the crags of Columbia's mountains.
They will fall on the lion with talons of steel,
   When the war-cry is raised by their brothers ;
They will strike, and the power of the tyrant shall
     reel
   'Neath the pangs he has meted to others.

Forget not the time when the spirit of Moore
   Like a tropic breeze moved in thy bowers,
And warmed every garden and glen of thy shore
   Till they blossomed with liberty's flowers ;

But languish not now for the summer of song, —
  Lo ! the autumn wind over thee rages ;
The fields are all ready, the reapers are strong,
  And they rush to the harvest of ages.

O Erin ! thy glorious hair mingles with gray,
  And thy blue eyes are swimming in sorrow,
But the millions who mock at thy visions to-day
  Shall view thee in wonder to-morrow :
Thou shalt rise from the anguish now rending thy
      breast,
  And hurl on the scoffer thy scorning ;
Thy night shall be lit by the stars of the West,
  Till it breaks into Freedom's full morning.

TWO CONQUERORS.

'Twas midnight on the tented plain,
  The din of strife had died away,
And, tangled in the lion's mane,
  The captive Corsican eagle lay;
No more, 'mid shouts of victory won,
  His pinions climbed the morning light, —
The splendor of his noonday sun
  Was quenched in swift and awful night;
They bore him in his iron cage
  To stern Helena's rock-walled shore,
To beat the bars with baffled rage
  In answer to the ocean's roar.
There, haunted by the orphan's shriek,
  The widow's curse, the mother's moan,
With battered wings and muzzled beak
  The bird of doom was left alone;
And when he died the pent-up wrath
  Of Nature burst in flame and flood,
As if to cleanse his blackened path
  Whose rule was born of woe and blood:
And Freedom will his name record
  With those who bore her name in vain, —

Who raised on high the victor's sword,
   But forged for man a tyrant's chain.

.   .   .   .

Oh, silent man, whose mighty deeds
   Awoke the land from dumb despair,
Who rose responsive to our needs
   In answer to a nation's prayer, —
Whose trustful manhood, warm and true,
   Through every act and impulse ran,
Till foes whom war could not subdue
   Surrendered to the kindly Man. —
Oh, Master of each storied field
   Where mortal man with thee has striven,
Till death itself was forced to yield
   And fly before thy faith in heaven:
When every battle-flag is furled,
   And love has wiped away our tears,
When songs of peace shall thrill the world,
   Thy life shall tower above the years
Like some calm mountain, crowned with snows
   Which o'er the storms of summer shine,
From whose green heart a river flows,
   And o'er whose feet the myrtles twine;
And Freedom's hand shall write thy name
   Among the few bright names of Time
That glow with all a conqueror's fame,
   Unclouded by a conqueror's crime.

THE OLD MOUNTAIN TREE.

OH ! the home we loved by the bounding deep,
   Where the hills in glory stood,
And the moss-grown graves, where our fathers sleep,
   'Neath the boughs of the waving wood;
We remember yet, with a fond regret
   For the rock and the flowery lea,
Where we once used to play through the long, long
      day,
   In the shade of the Old Mountain Tree.

We are pilgrims now, in stranger lands,
   And the joys of youth are passed;
Kind friends are gone, but the old tree stands
   Unharmed by the warring blast :
The lark may sing in the clouds of spring,
   And the swan on the silver sea,
But we long for the shade where the wild bird made
   Her nest in the Old Mountain Tree.

The time went by like a tale that's told,
   In a land of song and mirth,
And many a form in the churchyard cold
   Finds rest from the cares of earth;

And many a day shall wander away
    O'er the waves of the western sea,
And the heart will pine and vainly pray
    For a grave by the Old Mountain Tree.

THE ROVER'S GRAVE.

THEY bore him away when day had fled,
  And the storm was rolling high,
And they laid him down in his lonely bed
  By the light of an angry sky;
The lightning flashed, and the wild sea lashed
  The shore with its foaming wave,
And the thunder passed on the rushing blast,
  As it howled o'er the Rover's Grave.

No longer for him — like a fearless bird —
  Yon bark floats under the Lee,
No longer his voice on the gale is heard
  When its guns peal over the sea;
But near him the white gull builds on high
  Her nest by the gleaming wave,
And the heaving billows groan and die
  On the sands of the Rover's Grave.

THE ROCK OF LIBERTY.

A SONG for the rock, the stern old rock,
That braved the blast and the billows' shock;
It was born with Time on a barren shore,
And laughed with scorn at the breakers' roar!
'Twas here that first the Pilgrim band
Came weary up to the foaming strand;
And the tree they reared in those days gone by,
It lives, it lives, — and ne'er shall die!

Thou firm old rock, in the ages past
Thy brow was bleached by the warring blast;
But thy wintry toil with the wave is o'er,
And the billows beat thy base no more!
Yet countless as thy sands, old rock,
Are the hardy sons of the Pilgrim stock;
And the tree they reared in the days gone by,
It lives, it lives, — and ne'er shall die!

Then rest, old rock, on the sea-beat shore, —
Our sires are lulled by the ocean's roar!
'Twas here that first their hymns were heard,
O'er the startled cry of the white sea-bird!

'Twas here they lived, 'twas here they died, —
Their forms repose on the green hill's side;
But the tree they reared in the days gone by,
It lives, it lives, — and ne'er shall die !

MEET ME BY THE RUNNING BROOK.

MEET me by the running brook,
   Where the drooping willows grow;
Meet me in the shady nook,
   Where the silver waters flow.
Friends we loved are broken-hearted,
   Smiles have flown and tears have started
Since the time when last we parted,
   In the days of long ago.

Meet me when the starlight plays
   O'er the wavelets bright and low;
Tell me of our youthful days,
   E'er the heart knew pain or woe.
Joy will come to charm and leave us,
   Lingering hope will still deceive us;
Life had nothing dark to grieve us,
   In the days of long ago.

THE EXILE'S RETURN.

My mountain home, my own green hills,
   I see your long-lost glories rise,
I hear the birds and gushing rills
   That roam beneath your clear blue skies;
Ah! here I dwelt in early years,
   When hopes were high and hearts were true,
Ere love's bright dream was dimmed with tears,
   And life had lost its rainbow hue.

My mountain home, sweet home of yore,
   I left your paths in life's fair May,
And as I view their scenes once more
   I wipe the starting tear away:
They greet me not, the young, the old,
   The early loved of boyhood's bloom,
For years have rolled and hearts grown cold,
   And friends are sleeping in the tomb.
I see my home on yonder hill, —
The woods are waving o'er it still,
While far below the torrent shines
Like silver through the tow'ring pines.

JOYS OF MY CHILDHOOD.

Joys of my childhood,
Vanished forever,
Days oft remembered which never return,
Flowers in the wildwood
Path by the river,
Long will their memory linger and burn.
Dear was the home of my father and mother,
There have I played with my sister and brother,
There have I roamed by the side of another,
Happy and pure in my life's merry morn.

Friends of my childhood,
Tender and loving,
Scattered like leaves o'er the desolate plain,
Dreams of my childhood,
Where are ye roving,
Never to gladden my pathway of pain?
Morning that burns on the brow of the billow,
Driving the mist from the mariner's pillow,
Waking the lark from her nest 'neath the willow,
Brings not the light of my lost youth again.

OH! TAKE ME FROM THE FESTAL THRONG.

OH! take me from the festal throng,
  Where loving hearts grow false and cold,
And let me hear one burning song
  That thrilled my soul in days of old.
I may not feel that kindling flame,
  The trembling hope, the inward glow,
For dreams of beauty, love, and fame,
  Are faded lights of long ago.

There's not a tone in Nature's voice,
  There's not a ray by noon or night,
But lights the shrine of buried joys,
  Or tells a tale of lost delight, —
The morning sun, the moon's pale beam,
  The stars that shine with fainter glow,
And bird and breeze, and lake and stream,
  Bring back the forms of long ago.

Then take me from the festal throng,
  Where loving hearts grow false and cold,
And let me hear one burning song
  That thrilled my soul in days of old.

I cannot trace those winding ways
　Where life's young flowers no longer grow,
But, oh! I feel beneath thy gaze
　The morning light of long ago.

MOONLIGHT AND STARLIGHT.

FAR over ocean, o'er moorland and lea,
   Moonlight and starlight are beaming :
Wake from thy slumber, and wander with me
   Down where the roses are dreaming.
         Come to the hills,
          Sing with the rills,
   Roam where the river is shining ;
Oh, may our hopes, like the stars o'er the sea,
   Live when our day is declining.
Moonlight and starlight, silently beaming,
   Gilding the mountain, silving the wave,
Moonlight and starlight, tenderly streaming
   Over the beautiful, over the brave.

Daylight has flown to the caves of the deep,
   Mars o'er the mountain is burning;
Rise ere the song-birds awake from their sleep,
   Come ere the dawn is returning ;
         Sing me the lays
         Breathing of days
   Radiant with memories olden,
Sweet as the flowers where the night shadows weep,
   Pure as the moonbeams golden.
        Moonlight and starlight, etc.

OREANNA.

THE moon is on the sea, Oreanna,
I'm dreaming still of thee, Oreanna;
   The stars are in the skies,
   But I'm thinking of the eyes
That were more than all the stars of heaven to me.
   Shall I meet thee, Oreanna,
When life's evening shadows meet eternal day?
   Wilt thou know me, Oreanna,
In that morning light that never turns to gray?
   Oreanna, Oreanna.

The summer days go by, Oreanna,
The winters veil the sky, Oreanna;
   But winter's chilling gloom
   Cannot quench the light and bloom
Of that climate where the lilies never die.
   Shall I meet thee, Oreanna,
When life's weary winter melts in endless May?
   Wilt thou love me, Oreanna,
In that glowing spring that never dies away?
   Oreanna, Oreanna.

WE CANNOT GIVE THEE UP.

RETURN, dear one, return to-night,
  And cheer our lonely fold,
Bring back those hours of glad delight
  More dear than fame or gold.

CHORUS.

We cannot, cannot give thee up,
  We will not let thee go
To drown thy soul, and drain the cup
  Of ruin, shame, and woe.

Nay, by those bright departed days
  That gild our home no more,
That shine through memory's tender haze
  From memory's golden shore,
          We cannot, etc.

By Him who prayed and died for man,
  On Calvary's storied height,
Who took the hand of Magdalen
  And led her to the light,
          We cannot, etc.

The days seem dark when thou art gone,
The nights are filled with tears;
Return, dear one, and bring the dawn
Of happier, nobler years.
We cannot, etc.

THE CAPTIVE.

I AM dreaming of my home,
Of the valley where the torrent dashes by,
  Where the eagle and the wild deer love to roam,
And the mountains hang their shadows in the sky.

    I am grieving for the maid
Who will linger for her warrior in vain,
  She will listen for my signal in the shade,
And the footsteps that will never come again.

    I am bleeding far away
From the glories of my native mountain sky,
  And I'm longing in my bondage for the day
When the foe shall lead their captive forth to die.

    In my slumber I am free,
And, in dreams, again I grasp the bended bow;
  But I waken in my solitude to see
The vision melt in fetters and in woe.

SONG OF THE INDIAN MOTHER.

GENTLY dream, my darling child,
Sleeping in the lonely wild;
Would thy dreams might never know
Clouds that darken mine with woe;
Oh! to smile as thou art smiling,
All my hopeless hours beguiling
With the hope that thou mightst see
Blessings that are hid from me.

CHORUS.

Lullaby, my gentle boy,
  Sleeping in the wilderness,
Dreaming in thy childish joy
  Of a mother's fond caress, —
  Lullaby, lullaby.

Sleep, while gleams the council fire,
Kindled by thy hunted sire:
Guarded by thy God above,
Sleep and dream of peace and love:
Dream not of the band that perished
From the sacred soil they cherished,

Nor the ruthless race that roams
O'er our ancient shrines and homes.

Sleep, while autumn glories fly,
'Neath the melancholy sky,
From the trees before the storm,
Chased by winter's tyrant form :
Oh! 'tis thus our warriors, wasted,
From their altars torn and blasted,
Followed by the storm of death,
Fly before Oppression's breath.

Sleep, while night hides home and grave,
Rest, while mourn the suff'ring brave,
Mourning as thou, too, wilt mourn,
Through the future, wild and worn;
Bruised in heart, in spirit shaken,
Scourged by man, by God forsaken,
Wandering on in war and strife,
Living still, yet cursing life.

Could thy tender fancy feel
All that manhood will reveal,
Couldst thou dream thy breast would share
All the ills thy fathers bear,
Thou wouldst weep as I am weeping,
Tearful watches wildly keeping,
By the silver-beaming light
Of the long and lonely night.

MOONLIGHT HOURS.

WHEN moonlight hours in beauty beam
  Along the midnight shore,
I wander by the waves and dream
  Of hours that shine no more;
And then the tide of by-gone years
  Returns o'er life's blue sea,
Till from the rolling mist appears
  Each scene I loved with thee.

The moonlight hours may wane and fade
  From yonder changing sky,
The light of youth may turn to shade,
  And friendship's taper die, —
But let the skies be dark or bright
  That bend o'er life's blue sea,
My heart will view through day and night
  Each scene I loved with thee.

When moonlight hours their beams unite
  Along the murmuring main,
I dream beneath their melting light
  Of hearts that meet again:

The world may smile, and glory fling
　Its glance o'er scenes to be,
But still my heart will turn and cling
　To all I loved with thee.

HARRY O'LANE.

THE sunlight was streaming through woodbine and
   willow,
The clover was blooming on meadow and plain,
And a bark floated off like a bird o'er the billow,
   The morning I parted from Harry O'Lane,—
      Dear Harry O'Lane, lost Harry O'Lane.

The heavens grew dark, and I heard the wild warn-
   ing
That tells of a storm coming down on the main,
And I knew in my heart that the last golden morning
   Had dawned on the world for my Harry O'Lane,—
      Dear Harry O'Lane, lost Harry O'Lane.

The wing of the blast o'er the ocean came sweeping,
   I knelt to the God of the sailor in vain,
And I dream of a form on the red coral sleeping,
   Where foundered the bark of my Harry O'Lane,—
      Dear Harry O'Lane, lost Harry O'Lane.

The morning winds play through the bright golden
   willows,
   I hear the glad music of waters again,

But never shall morning, nor breezes, nor billows,
Bring back the glad voice of my Harry O'Lane, —
Dear Harry O'Lane, lost Harry O'Lane.

'TIS SWEET TO BE REMEMBERED.

OH! 'tis sweet to be remembered
  In the merry days of youth,
While the world seems full of brightness,
  And the soul retains its truth;
When our hopes are like the morning beams
  That flash along the sea,
And every dream we know of life
  Is one of purity;
'Tis sweet to be remembered
  As the spring remembers earth,
Spreading roses in our pathway,
  Filling all our hearts with mirth.

Oh! 'tis sweet to be remembered
  In the summer-time of life,
Ere we reach the burning summit
  With our weight of woe and strife;
To look backward through the shadows
  Where our journey first begun,
And the golden flowers of memory
  Turn their faces to the sun;
'Tis sweet to be remembered,
  As the breeze remembers day,

Floating upward from the valley,
 O'er the pilgrim's weary way.

Oh! 'tis sweet to be remembered
 When our life has lost its bloom,
And every morning sun we meet
 May leave us at the tomb;
When our youth is half forgotten,
 And we gaze with yearnings fond
From a world where all is dying
 To a deathless world beyond;
'Tis sweet to be remembered,
 As the stars remember night,
Shining downward through the darkness,
 With a pure and holy light.

SLEEP, ROBIN, SLEEP.

SLEEP, Robin, sleep,
   While mother watches o'er you,
And bright starry skies
   Bend o'er the sleeping land.
Rest, birdie, rest;
   The world is all before you,
And pleasure and pain
   Go ever hand in hand.

Sleep, Robin, sleep,
   With mother's wing above you,
And soft angel eyes
   To guard your sleeping form.
Rest, birdie, rest;
   May angels ever love you,
And walk by your side
   In sunshine and in storm.

CHORUS.

Sleep, Robin, lullaby;
   Rest, birdie, lullaby;
Sleep, sleep, Robin, lullaby.

LET US LOVE WHILE WE MAY.

LET us love while we may, for the storms will arise
    As we sail o'er the blue waves of Time,
And the hopes of to-day may be hid from our eyes
    By the noon-clouds that darken our prime.
We may look for the lost hills of morning, and
        grieve,
    But the soft hush of twilight will come,
And our souls on the rose-tinted billows of eve
    Float calmly away to their home.

Let us love while we live, and our mem'ry will rise
    Like a halo of light from the grave,
As the day from the deep lends a glow to the eyes
    That are guarding the gloom of the wave.
There's a life in the soul that is better by far
    Than the glitter of glory and gold, —
It may fade in the noon, but will shine like a star
    When the proud world is darksome and cold.

MARION MOORE.

GONE art thou, Marion, Marion Moore, —
Gone like the bird in the autumn that singeth,
Gone like the flower by the wayside that springeth,
Gone like the leaf of the ivy that clingeth
    Round the lone rock on a storm-beaten shore.

Dear wert thou, Marion, Marion Moore, —
Dear as the tide in my broken heart throbbing;
Dear as the soul o'er thy memory sobbing.
Sorrow my life of its roses is robbing,
    Wasting is all the glad beauty of yore.

I will remember thee, Marion Moore, —
I shall remember, alas, to regret thee;
I will regret when all others forget thee;
Deep in my breast will the hour that I met thee
    Linger and burn till life's fever is o'er.

Gone art thou, Marion, Marion Moore, —
Gone like the breeze o'er the billow that bloweth,
Gone as the rill, to the ocean that floweth,
Gone as the day from the gray mountain goeth,
    Darkness behind thee, but glory before.

Peace to thee, Marion, Marion Moore, —
Peace which the queens of the earth cannot borrow,
Peace from a kingdom that crowned thee with sor-
    row :
Oh ! to be happy with thee on the morrow,
  Who would not fly from this desolate shore ?

LORD, KEEP MY MEMORY GREEN.

My feet approach life's western slope :
   Above me bend the noonday skies,
Beyond me spreads the realm of hope,
   Behind, the land of memory lies ;
I know not what the years may bring
   Of dangers wild, or joys serene ;
But, turning to the east, I sing,
   " Lord, keep my memory green."

O land of winter and of bloom,
   Of singing bird, and moaning pine,
Thy golden light, thy tender gloom,
   Thy vales and mountains, all are mine !
The holy loves of other years,
   With beck'ning hands toward me lean,
And whisper, through their falling tears,
   " Lord, keep my memory green."

Dear Memory ! whose unclouded gaze
   Can pierce the darkest wilds of space,
I see her morning watch-fires blaze,
   I feel her breezes fan my face ;

I would not give the light she flings
  Across my future's landscape scene
For all the pomp and power of kings, —
  " Lord, keep my memory green."

Let Mémory near my soul abide,
  With eye and voice to warn and win,
Till Hope and Memory, side by side,
  Shall walk above the tides of sin, —
Till from life's western lakes and rills
  The angel lifts the sunset sheen,
And hangs it o'er the eastern hills, —
  " Lord, keep my memory green."

THE MOUNTAINS OF LIFE.

THERE's a land far away mid the stars, we are told,
　Where they know not the sorrows of time;
Where the pure waters wander through valleys of
　　gold,
　And life is a treasure sublime :
'Tis the land of our God, 'tis the home of the soul,
Where ages of splendor eternally roll,
Where the way-weary traveller reaches his goal
　On the evergreen mountains of life.

Our gaze cannot soar to that beautiful land,
　But our visions have told of its bliss;
And our souls by the gales from its gardens are
　　fanned
　When we faint in the deserts of this;
And we sometimes have longed for its holy repose
When our spirits were torn with temptations and
　　woes,
And we've drunk from the tide of the river that flows
　From the evergreen mountains of life.

Oh ! the stars never tread the blue heavens at night
　But we think where the ransomed have trod;

And the day never smiles from his palace of light
  But we feel the bright smile of our God.
We are travelling homeward, through changes and
      gloom,
To a kingdom where pleasures unceasingly bloom,
And our guide is the glory that shines through the
      tomb,
  From the evergreen mountains of life.

THE DAWN OF REDEMPTION.

SEE them go forth like the floods of the ocean,
　Gathering might from each mountain and glen;
Wider and deeper the tide of devotion
　Rolls up to God from the bosoms of men;
Hear the great multitude singing in chorus,
　Groan as they gaze from their crimes to the sky,
Father, the midnight of death gathers o'er us,
　When will the dawn of redemption draw nigh?"

"Look on us wanderers, sinful and lowly,
　Struggling with grief and temptation below;
Thine is the goodness o'er every thing holy,
　Thine is the mercy to pity our woe;
Thine is the power to cleanse and restore us
　Spotless and pure as the angels on high, —
"Father, the midnight of death gathers o'er us,
　When will the dawn of redemption draw nigh?"

Gray hair and golden youth, matron and maiden,
　Lovers of mammon and followers of fame,
All with the same solemn burden are laden,
　Lifting their souls to that one mighty name, —

"Wild is the pathway that surges before us,
   On the broad waters the black shadows lie ;
Father, the midnight of death gathers o'er us,
   When will the dawn of redemption draw nigh?"

Lo! the vast depths of futurity's ocean
   Heave with the pulse of the Infinite breath,
Why should we shrink from the billows' commotion?
   Angels are walking the waters of death ;
Angels are blending their notes in the chorus,
   Rising like incense from earth to the sky, —
"Father, the billows grow lighter before us,
   Heaven with its mansions eternal draws nigh."

THE BEAUTIFUL HILLS.

OH! the Beautiful Hills where the blest have trod
 Since the years when the earth was new:
Where our fathers gaze from the fields of God
 On the vale we are journeying through:
We have seen those hills in their brightness rise
 When the world was black below,
And we felt the thrill of immortal eyes
 In the night of our darkest woe.
  Then sing of the Beautiful Hills,
   That rise from the evergreen shore;
  Oh! sing of the Beautiful Hills,
   Where the weary shall toil no more.

The cities of yore that were reared in crime,
 And renowned by the praise of seers,
Went down in the tramp of old King Time,
 To sleep with his gray-haired years;
But the Beautiful Hills rise bright and strong
 Through the smoke of old Time's red wars,
As on that day when the first deep song
 Rolled up from the morning stars.
  Then sing of the Beautiful Hills, etc.

We dream of rest on the Beautiful Hills,
    Where the traveller shall thirst no more ;
And we hear the hum of a thousand rills
    That wander the green glens o'er.
We can feel the souls of the martyred men
    Who have braved a cold world's frown ;
We can bear the burdens which they did then,
    Nor shrink from their thorny crown.
        Then sing of the Beautiful Hills, etc.

Our arms are weak, yet we would not fling
    To our feet this load of ours.
The winds of spring to the valleys sing,
    And the turf replies with flowers ;
And thus we learn on our wintry way
    How a mightier arm controls,
That the breath of God on our lives will play
    Till our bodies bloom to souls.
        Then sing of the Beautiful Hills, etc.

PROPHET OF NAZARETH.

SWEET prophet of Nazareth, constant and tender,
   Whose truth like a rainbow encircles the world;
The time is approaching when wrong shall surrender,
   And war's crimson banners forever be furled;
When the throat of the lion no longer shall utter
   Its roar of defiance in desert and glen,
When the lands will join hands, and the black can-
      non mutter
   Their discords no more to the children of men.
As breaks the gold sunlight, when heroes and sages
   Were rising and falling like meteors in space,
A new glory broke on the gloom of the ages,
   And love warmed to life in the glow of thy face;
The wars of the Old Time are waning and failing,
   The peace of the New Time o'erarches our tears,
The orbs of the Old Time are fading and paling,
   The sun of the New Time is gilding the years.

The mist of the ocean, the spray of the fountain,
   The vine on the hillside, the moss on the shrine,
The rose in the valley, the pine on the mountain,
   All turn to a glory that symboleth thine;

So I yearn for thy love as the purest and dearest
  That ever uplifted a spirit from woe,
And I turn to Thy life as the truest and nearest
  To Infinite Goodness that mortals may know.

O Soul of the Orient, peerless and holy,
  Enthroned in a splendor all angels above,
I would join with the singers that raise up the lowly,
  And praise Thee in deeds that are Christlike in
    love.
Let my words be as showers that fall on the high-
    lands,
  Begotten in shadows, expiring in light,
While Thine are the billows that sing to life's islands
  In numbers unbroken, by noonday and night.

WHERE THE ROSES NEVER WITHER.

WHERE the roses ne'er shall wither,
Nor the clouds of sorrow gather,
 We shall meet, we shall meet :
Where no wintry storm can roll,
Driving summer from the soul ;
Where all hearts are tuned to love,
On that happy shore above.

CHORUS.

Where the roses ne'er shall wither,
Nor the storms of sorrow gather,
Angel bands will guide us thither,
Where the roses ne'er shall wither.

Where the hills are ever vernal,
And the springs of youth eternal,
 We shall meet, we shall meet :
Where life's morning dream returns,
And the noonday never burns ;
Where the dew of life is love,
On that happy shore above.

Where no cruel word is spoken,
Where no faithful heart is broken,
　　We shall meet, we shall meet:
Hand in hand and heart to heart,
Friend with friend, no more to part,
Ne'er to grieve for those we love,
On that happy shore above.

MY PRAYER.

FATHER, bend Thine ear and hear me
  While I call to Thee in prayer,
Let Thine angels linger near me
  In my time of grief and care, —
Like the sun upon the river
  Let thy love upon me shine,
Till my life shall sing forever
  In the boundlesss deep of Thine.

Father, when my lips are pleading
  For the weary march to end,
Homeless, lonely, torn, and bleeding,
  Let me find in Thee a friend;
When like leaves my hopes are falling,
  And despair has filled my breast,
Let me hear Thy low voice calling, —
  "Come, and I will give you rest."

Father, let Thy spirit guide me
  Through the darkness and the blast,
Let Thine angels walk beside me,
  Till temptation's power be past, —

Till I view the heights supernal
  Tow'ring o'er life's changing sea,
Till I tread the vales eternal,
  Where the blest are led by Thee.

THE ISLES OF THE BY AND BY.

WE shall meet again in the By and By,
Where the mountains gleam in the morning sky,
We shall meet again in the land of Love,
Our Father's home above.

CHORUS.

We shall meet again, we shall meet again,
  In the beautiful Isles of the By and By,
We shall meet again, we shall meet again,
  In the Isles of the By and By.

In the balmy Isles where the angels roam
By the crystal seas of our Father's Home,
There are forms of grace and of beauty rare,
And the ones we have lost are there.

We must part in tears when the twilight dies
On the far-off hills of our evening skies;
We shall meet in joy where our dear ones stand
In the gates of the Morning Land.

We shall fall asleep where the autumn grieves
O'er the fading flowers and the falling leaves ;
We shall wake again where the angels sing
In the bloom of eternal spring.

BEAUTIFUL ANNIE.

BEAUTIFUL Annie, silver-voiced Annie,
  Gone ere thy light heart knew sorrow and woe;
Beautiful Annie, silver-voiced Annie,
  Oh, how we miss thee no mortal may know!
Sweet is thy song, though the world may not hear it;
Bright is thy home, with the angels to cheer it;
Oh, for one view of thy glorified spirit,
  Free from the fetters that bind us below!

Beautiful Annie, silver-voiced Annie,
  Gone ere thy young life a shadow might feel;
Beautiful Annie, silver-voiced Annie,
  Green is thy memory in sorrow and weal:
Thine is the splendor of joy undeceiving,
Ours be the love to thy memory cleaving,
Ours be the faith which is blest in believing
  All the fond visions the angels reveal.

Beautiful Annie, silver-voiced Annie,
  Gone from our pathway in life's early May;
Beautiful Annie, silver-voiced Annie,
  Smile on our home from thy glory-lit way.

Glide round the hearts that so oft were thy pillow,
Sing in our gloom like the bird in the willow,
Come to our night like the star to the billow,
  Gilding the wave with a promise of day.

CHILDREN'S DAY.

THE wintry winds have flown away
　　To colder lands than ours,
And summer brings this joyous day
　　With all its wealth of flowers ;
We come in many a happy throng,
　　We meet in every clime,
To crown with love and cherful song
　　The dearest name of Time.

REFRAIN.

We come, we come,
　　Amid the bloom of June ;
Our hearts are light,
Our faces bright,
　　Our voices all in tune ;
We come, we come,
　　Our love for Him to prove
Who took the children in His arms,
　　And blest them with His love.

Let lilies breathe and roses fling
　　Their fragrance on the air,

And all the birds of summer sing
  In one melodious prayer;
Let mountain, river, rill, and lake
  Give praises to His name,
And every voice of Nature wake
  Our hearts to holy flame.

LOOK UP.

Look up, look up, desponding soul,
   The clouds are only seeming,
The light behind the dark'ning scroll
   Eternally is beaming.
     Wait on, hope on,
     Work with heart and hand;
Make room in your life for the angel throng
     From the beautiful morning land.

The warmth and glow of deathless youth
   Shall crown the true endeavor;
The tide of God's immortal truth
   Climbs up and on forever.

There is no death, there is no night,
   Nor life nor day declining;
Beyond the day's departing light
   The sun is always shining.

Could we but pierce the rolling storms
   That veil the pathway sunward,
We'd see a host of shining forms
   Forever beckoning onward.

LEONA.

LEONA, the hour draws nigh, —
The hour we've awaited so long,
For the angel to open a door through the sky,
That my spirit may break from its prison and try
Its voice in an infinite song.

Just now, as the slumbers of night
Came o'er me with peace-giving breath,
The curtain, half lifted, revealed to my sight
Those windows which look on the kingdon of light
That borders the River of Death.

And a vision fell solemn and sweet,
Bringing gleams of a morning-lit land ;
I saw the white shore which the pale waters beat,
And I heard the low lull as they broke at their feet
Who walked on the beautiful strand.

And I wondered why spirits should cling
To their clay with a struggle and sigh,
When life's purple autumn is better than spring,
And the soul flies away like a sparrow, to sing
In a climate where leaves never die.

Leona, come close to my bed,
    And lay your dear hand on my brow;
The same touch that thrilled me in days that are
    fled,
And raised the lost roses of youth from the dead,
    Can brighten the brief moments now.

We have loved from the cold world apart;
    And your trust was too generous and true
For their hate to o'erthrow: when the slanderer's
    dart
Was rankling deep in my desolate heart,
    I was dearer than ever to you.

I thank the Great Father for this,
    That our love is not lavished in vain;
Each germ, in the future, will blossom to bliss,
And the forms that we love, and the lips that we
    kiss,
    Never shrink at the shadow of pain.

By the light of this faith am I taught
    That death is but action begun;
In the strength of this hope have I struggled and
    fought
With the legions of wrong, till my armor has caught
    The gleam of Eternity's sun.

Leona, look forth and behold!
    From headland, from hillside, and deep,
The day king surrenders his banners of gold;

The twilight advances through woodland and wold,
    And the dews are beginning to weep.

The moon's silver hair lies uncurled,
    Down the broad-breasted mountains away;
Ere sunset's red glories again shall be furled
On the walls of the west, o'er the plains of the world,
    I shall rise in a limitless day.

Oh! come not in tears to my tomb,
    Nor plant with frail flowers the sod:
There is rest among roses too sweet for its gloom,
And life where the lilies eternally bloom,
    In the balm-breathing gardens of God.

Yet deeply those memories burn
    Which bind me to you and to earth;
And I sometimes have thought that my being would
    yearn,
In the bowers of its beautiful home, to return
    And visit the home of its birth.

'Twould even be pleasant to stay,
    And walk by your side to the last;
But the land-breeze of Heaven is beginning to play,
Life's shadows are meeting Eternity's day,
    And its tumult is hushed in the past.

Leona, good-by. Should the grief
    That is gathering now ever be

Too dark for your faith, you will long for relief ;
And, remember, the journey, though lonesome, is
    brief,
        Over lowland and river, to me.

THE GUARDIAN ANGEL.

I COME not from the weeping willow-tree :
    I sing of climes where pleasures ever thrill,
I bear a message of a life to be,
    When spheres dissolve, and warring waves are
        still ;
I guard thee in the early morning light,
    The noonday glare, the glow that paints the west ;
I gaze upon thee in the lonely night,
    And mark each sigh that stirs thy sleeping breast.

'Tis mine to hover near thee every hour ;
    To note the cares that shade thy troubled face,
Till life anew shall lift the fallen flower,
    And crown with deathless bloom each fading
        grace.
Though life seems dark, and hope shines dim and
        far,
    Faint not ; I never leave thee long alone : —
The golden light that speaks from star to star,
    Is far less fleet than love that claims its own.

GOING HOME.

Kiss me when my spirit flies, —
Let the beauty of your eyes
Beam along the waves of death
While I draw my parting breath,
And am borne to yonder shore
Where the billows beat no more,
And the notes of endless spring
Through the groves immortal ring.

I am going home to-night,
Out of blindness into sight,
Out of weakness, war, and pain,
Into power, peace, and gain,
Out of winter gale and gloom
Into summer breath and bloom;
From the wand'rings of the past
I am going home at last.

Kiss my lips and let me go:
Nearer swells the solemn flow
Of the wondrous stream that rolls
By the borderland of souls;

I can catch sweet strains of songs
Floating down from distant throngs,
And can feel the touch of hands
Reaching out from angel bands.

Anger's frown and envy's thrust,
Friendship chilled by cold distrust,
Sleepless night and weary morn,
Toil in fruitless land forlorn,
Aching head and breaking heart,
Love destroyed by slander's dart,
Drifting ship and darkened sea,
Over there will righted be.

Sing in numbers low and sweet,
Let the songs of two worlds meet,
We shall not be sundered long, —
Like the fragments of a song,
Like the branches of a rill
Parted by the rock or hill,
We shall blend in tune or time,
Loving on in perfect rhyme.

When the noontide of your days
Yields to twilight's silver haze,
Ere the world recedes in space,
Heavenward lift your tender face;
Let your dear eyes homeward shine,
Let your spirit call for mine,
And my own will answer you
From the deep and boundless blue.

Swifter than the sunbeam's flight
I will cleave the gloom of night,
And will guide you to the land
Where our loved ones waiting stand,
And the legions of the blest
There shall welcome you to rest;
They will know you when your eyes
On the isles of glory rise.

When the parted streams of life
Join beyond all jarring strife,
And the flowers that withered lay
Blossom in immortal May;
When the voices hushed and dear
Thrill once more the raptured ear,
We shall feel, and know, and see,
God knew better far than we.

OUR DREAM BY THE RIVER.

'TWAS here that we wandered when winter was over,
　And saw the white apple-blooms falling like snow,
The birds in the trees and the bees in the clover
　Were tuning their notes to the water's soft flow;
The earth was awaiting the birth of her roses,
　When all her sweet voices in harmony sing.
I shall never forget, till the day of life closes,
　Our dream by the river that morning in spring.

The soul of that morning still lingers in splendor,
　The song of the water still rings in my ears,
That look in your eyes, half reproachful yet tender,
　Has haunted my life through a long night of
　　　years;
On the vast rolling plains where the rivers pressed
　　onward
　For freedom and rest in the fetterless blue,
On the wonderful heights where the mountains swept
　　sunward
　I've paused to remember that morning and you.

THE PICTURE.

It was only a symbol in soft light and shade
Which the sun looking down in his glory had made,
But the sight of it touched me that morning in May
As a billow is touched by the birth of the day;
The landscape of Life at my feet lay unrolled,
Its rivers of silver, its sunsets of gold;
I heard the spring torrent rush down from the hill,
And, faint from the lowlands, the wood-robin's trill.

COMPLETENESS.

O LOVE that all my being warms!
O love that shields my life from storms!
O love that every impulse wills,
And every flitting fancy fills!
O love that shines through all my dreams
Like starlight through the summer streams;
That thrills with melody my days,
And rounds all discord into praise!—
I lean my face upon thy breast
As bends my noon-ray to the west,
And calmly, in my open boat,
I floating sing and singing float.
I wait no more by wayside lakes,
To dally with the reeds and brakes;
Behind me fade the mountain snows,
And in my face the June wind blows,
While strong and wide the currents sweep
Toward the ever-calling deep.
O love that rocks me in its arms,
And makes me brave amidst alarms!
I know not where thy stream may lead,
Through rocky pass or flowery mead,
I only feel that I am blest;
I only know I am at rest.

THE GOLDEN DREAM.

THE golden dream of all my life
   Is framed in soft September's ray,
And rises o'er long leagues of strife
   Like some blest island far away;
Its memory has haunted me,
When love seemed like a leafless tree,
   And charmed away my pain, love,
   And sung within my brain, love,
Like music from a moonlit sea.

O queen of all my royal hours,
   Before your glance all sorrow flies,
Your face looks out from stars and flowers,
   And lends new grace to hills and skies;
No more I tread the barren strands,
Through lonely wastes of burning sands,
   I walk no more in gloom, love,
   My life is glad with bloom, love,
And all its wealth is in your hands.

My every thought, in woe or weal,
   Across your soul some token flings,

And every new-born hope you feel
  In my own spirit soars and sings;
The love that leaps from soul to soul
Whose impulse Fate could not control,
  Shall conquer Time and Art, love,
  Shall hold us heart to heart, love,
When Time's brief years no longer roll.

My life is yours, your life is mine;
  Like crystal waters interwove,
No mortal will can fix a line
  To part the mingled tides of love:
The storms that vex the ocean's face,
Can only mar its outward grace,
  While calm below its crest, love,
  Deep down within its breast, love,
The waves are lulled in love's embrace.

LOVE'S MORNING CALL.

COME over the valley, my darling, my own,
  The flowers are waking in gladness and dew,
The spirit of night has deserted its throne,
    There's a blush of delight on the mountain's dark
      blue;
The arrows of morning are winging their way
    From a quiver of gold on the billow's broad
      breast,
The isles of the ocean are purpling with day,
  The moon lies asleep at the gates of the west.

I've seen the wild waters encompass your form
    As you reached in the darkness for comfort and
      light,
I've heard your low call in the din of the storm,
  And felt your soft touch in the stillness of night;
Your life shall forget all the anguish it bore
  When adrift and alone on a desolate deep;
The phantom of sorrow shall haunt you no more
  'Mid the cares of the day nor in visions of sleep.

Oh! love is of being the glory and grace,
  The power, the impulse, the voice, and the breath!

It can rest in the light of a dearly loved face,
  Yet is stronger than edict and ruler o'er death ;
If planets and systems between us should roll,
  And our paths by the spaces be sundered apart,
I should know when a shadow swept over your soul,
  And be swayed by the innermost pulse of your
    heart.

Come out from the lowlands, my beautiful one,
  I've crossed the dark mountains that hid you
    from me ;
The young morning's laugh ripples up from the sun,
  And dimples with smiles the sad face of the sea ;
From the highlands of gold to the valleys of green
  The voices of summer are singing in tune,
And roses are waiting to welcome the queen
  With their red lips upturned for the kisses of
    June.

I CARE NOT FOR THIS WORLD WITH-
OUT THEE.

I CARE not for this world without thee,
    Apart from thee all life is pain,
The flowers that bloom and breathe about me,
    If thou art gone, unfold in vain :
The sun and the moon, the twilight, the dawn,
Grow dim if the light of thy love be withdrawn ;
    Ah ! never can my spirit doubt thee
      While hope and trust and life remain.

CHORUS.

Oh ! hear me, hear me when I call thee,
When the moon is on the mountain beaming,
    Or the stars are dreaming
      Where the billows roll, —
    Ill cannot befall me
      While thou art near my soul.

Let other friends betray and leave me,
    And tears of bitter anguish fall,
I know one light will not deceive me,
    I know one ear will hear my call :

The sun may expire, the bright stars decay,
But thou wilt draw nearer while worlds fade away,
  Ah! never more can mortal grieve me,
    While dwells thine image over all.

CHORUS.

Oh! hear me, etc.

NIGHT ON THE PRAIRIE.

I AM here again, where the prairies sweep
Like the rolling tides of a shoreless deep;
And I eastward turn, while the clear, bright eyes
Of the planets flash in the midnight skies;
For dearer than all the orbs that shine
From the Milky Way to the world's low line,
Is one whose eyes are awaiting me
Behind the gates of the eastern sea.

Far up and away in the starry heights
Are the changing spires of the wild north lights,
As they form and fade, then gather again,
Like the sheen of spears on the battle plain,
Like the gleam of crests through the awful gloom
Where the Arctic monsters crash and boom,
And the uncurbed ice-steeds plunge and tramp
O'er the sentry lines of the storm-god's camp.

I am all alone in the waning night:
I have lingered here in the growing light
Till the stars have paled, and the skies turned gray
In the westward march of the coming day;

And lo! my beautiful Morning Star
Climbs over the brown horizon bar
And beckons to me from the verge of space
With the soul of day in her tender face.

LOVE'S IMMORTALITY.

OH, the gladness and glory
    Of life and of time
When love's dual story
    Is told in one rhyme !
When one face is pictured on brain and on eye,
And one name is written on rainbow and sky;
When the robins sing love through all seasons and
        changes,
And waves whisper love in the arms of the night;
When the years rise before us like green mountain
        ranges,
Whose cedars and myrtles are bathed in one light.

Like the rose by the fountain
    That mirrors its hue,
Like the rain on the mountain
    That hungers for dew,
So your life in the stream of my life saw its own,
So your presence brought flowers where no flowers
        had blown.
Oh, the clasp of our souls was the glory of living !
We shared with each other in pleasure and pain,

For the wealth of our love was the rapture of giving,
And all that we gave was the sweetest of gain.

Like the sun to the ocean
Where two vessels glide,
Keeping time to one motion
Of breeze and of tide,
Was the spell of our love to life's billow and air,
And in sorrow and shadow we knew it was there:
We knew it at midnight by stars shining o'er us,
When mist hid the deep, by a voice and a breath
Floating ever above and behind and before us,
A presence in darkness, in trial, and death.

How it sang through all weather
In mind and in heart!
How it willed us together
When sundered apart!
How the sweet star of Hope cast her smile on the
strife
Where the surges of fate shook the headlands of
life !
The landscapes of time have their Junes and De-
cembers,
And rivers of beauty between them that roll,
But of all that my spirit beholds or remembers,
Our love is the warmth, and the light, and the soul.

It may pass like the shower
That watered the earth;

It may fade like the flower
    That springtime gave birth;
The sun may go down on its gladness and bloom,
And the winter storm shroud it in drift and in gloom;
But the rain shall live on in the heart of the river,
The rose tint ascend to the cloud and the sky;
And the love that is ours shall enfold us forever,
When fountain, and river, and ocean are dry.

JUNE DAYS.

THE Queen of all the year
　　Once more walks land and sea;
Her days of bloom are here,
　　To tell my soul of thee:
The dearest days of all I know
　　In summer shade or shine,
For in their soft light long ago
　　A soul was born for mine.
O royal June!
Sweet flowering June!
Her song is in the rill
　　That to the valley flows,
Her tender eyes
Light earth and skies,
　　Her cheek with beauty glows,
Her breath perfumes the hill,
　　Her lips are in the rose.

And though we walked apart
　　Till life's brief May was o'er,
The summer of the heart
　　Is ours forevermore.

And so the Junes are ever new,
   And filled with glad surprise,
For all their bloom, their light and dew,
   Are blended in thine eyes.
O royal June!
Sweet flowering June!
Her song is in the rill
   That to the valley flows,
Her tender eyes
Light earth and skies,
   Her cheek with beauty glows,
Her breath perfumes the hill,
   Her lips are in the rose.

THE WOMAN IN THE MOON.

O MOON ! that from your starry height
   Looks down on river, lake, and sea,
Go seek her eyes whose tender light
   Is more than star and sun to me ;
Reflect on thine the radiant face
   That cheered my way when all was dark,
And send the picture down through space
   To light the tide that bears my bark.

Ah, moon ! I see her image now
   Reflected on thy silver shield,
It sways before my vessel's prow, —
   The fairest wave and sky can yield.
I see her face in beauty rise,
   And, o'er the changing glance of thine,
The steadfast glory of her eyes
   Is beaming fondly into mine.

OUR LOVE SHALL NEVER DIE.

No matter where my feet may stand,
On silent plain or noisy strand,
On sailing ship or solid land,
In lowly ways or mountains grand,
  My soul is close to you, love,
  My soul is close to you.

No matter what my lips may say
To turn the questioning world away,
In moments sad, in moments gay,
In clouded night or cloudless day,
  My life to you is true, love,
  My life to you is true.

The morning suns may lose their gold,
The bright warm noons turn pale and cold,
And all bright things we now behold
In earth and air and wave, grow old,
  And fade from brain and eye, love,
  And fade from brain and eye.

But in the gloom of deepest night
A rose shall wave in beauty bright,

A star shall hail the morning light,
A bird shall sing across the night,
  "Our love shall never die, love,
  Our love shall never die."

VENUS.

WHEN Venus rises from the deep
   With morning glory in her face,
And all her train have gone to sleep
   Behind the paling dome of space,
Sweet mem'ries through my being sweep
   Of one whose rare and loving grace
Flung o'er my dark and lonely way
A promise of the coming day.

When Venus from her throne of blue
   Stoops down to touch the western sea,
Before her train appears in view
   From out the calm Immensity,
I turn to her, and think of you,
   Whose love is life and light to me,
Whose touch controlled my troubled breast,
And gave me peace for wild unrest.

I WILL BE WITH YOU.

I will be with you when daylight is ending,
   And sunset's rare glories have died on the plain,
When Love's evening star from her throne is descend-
      ing,
   To lave her sweet face in the foam of the main.

I will be with you when cold dews are falling,
   And song-birds have ceased to remember the day,
When dark rolling waves through the midnight are
      calling
   For stars to come down and illumine the way.

I will be with you when daylight is breaking,
   And dawn's tender promise is kindling the skies,
When Love's morning star in the east is awaking
   With new life and light in her beautiful eyes,
         I will be with you,
         I will be with you,
         On sea and shore, —
         I will be with you,
         I will be with you,
           Forevermore.

THE BOATMAN'S DREAM.

WITH long arm o'er the prairies tossed,
  And feet that bathed in tropic spray,
And head all white with Northern frost,
  The mighty Sire of Waters lay:
His fingers gleamed with priceless mines,
  Or watered herds along the plains,
And lowly grass and lofty pines
  Drew life and grandeur from his veins.

The June winds left their mountain towers
  Which guard the Valleys of the West,
With odors from a million flowers
  To soothe the sleeping giant's rest;
They danced along his pulsing form,
  With many a quaint and charming grace,
And threw their kisses, sweet and warm,
  In dimples on his quiet face.

It was the time when human souls
  Their visioned thoughts of Heaven renew,
And inspiration o'er us rolls
  From rising star and falling dew:

The hour when higher aims have birth,
    And passion's wildest tides are still, —
When angel pinions fan the earth,
    And men may feel them if they will.

An humble boatman viewed the scene
    In silence from his crew apart,
As, slowly through the twilight sheen,
    His rude craft sought the Southern mart;
And o'er him swayed a form of light,
    Unseen, but felt in soul and mind;
As lightning glimmers through the night,
    Vivid and clear, yet undefined.

A black man hummed a careless air,
    And toiled to swell a white man's gains,
And little dreamed the boatman there
    Would yet redeem his race from chains.
With folded arm and pensive eye
    The boatman gazed upon the stream;
And, lo! the spell of prophecy
    Stole on his senses like a dream.

And, like the sound of far-off floods,
    When ocean choirs majestic roll
Their wild psalms through the mellowing woods,
    A low voice murmured to his soul.
And sweeter than the hymns of birds
    Which thrill the springtime of the year,
That low voice, melting into words,
    Thus sank upon his dreaming ear:

"O'er highlands green and billows blue
  I bear the banner of the Free,
I am the Genius of the True,
  The glorious Maid of Liberty;
I led the Pilgrim to the rock,
  I tuned the soul of William Tell;
I live in every battle shock
  That rings the key to Slavery's knell.

"God gave a New World to thy sires,
  When despots trampled on the Old;
And I in Truth's eternal fires
  Baptized a nation for my fold:
I took it from the lion's grasp,
  And fondly nursed its wondrous charms:
I held it with a mother's clasp,
  And guided it through war's alarms.

"And I have loved it since the time
  Of Lexington and Bunker Hill;
I've warned it of the Old World's crime,
  I pray that God may shield it still;
But God is just, and time is sure,
  And vengeance will arise at last,
To crush the crime it cannot cure,
  In sword and fire and cannons' blast.

"What though the palm tree smite the pine,
  And Saxon's first recoil with pain?
The Serpent of the South will twine
  Around the Eagle's nest in vain.

Its folds shall know the squadrons' tread,
　　The burning town, the combats' glare,
While Mercy bows her golden head,
　　And shuts her blue eyes in despair.

"Go forth, sad man of thought and care,
　　Of weary nights and anxious morns;
'Tis thine to toil, and wait and wear,
　　Mid sneers and taunts, the crown of thorns.
But those who curse thee most shall bow
　　And bless thy work in brighter hours;
The crown shall blossom on thy brow,
　　And all its thorns be changed to flowers.

"Thy people do not know thee; yet,
　　In yon black night that looms afar,
When all thy earthly hopes have set,
　　Thy name will be their morning star:
And by its light a race of slaves
　　Will march as did the slaves of yore,
Unfettered through the Red Sea waves,
　　Triumphant to the Promised Shore."

The full moon climbed the skies of June
　　To hang her shield on lake and stream;
The river played a pleasant tune,
　　And woke the boatman from his dream.
And when the Junes of many years
　　Had bloomed and ripened in the land,
A nation placed, mid hopes and fears,
　　Its sceptre in the boatman's hand.

With life unsullied from his youth
   He meekly took the ruler's rod;
And, wielding it in love and truth,
   He lived, "the noblest work of God."
He knew no fierce, unbalanced zeal,
   That spurns all human differings,
Nor craven fear which shuns the steel
   That carves the way to better things.

And in the night of blood and grief,
   When horror rested on the Ark,
His was the calm, undimmed belief
   That felt God's presence in the dark.
Full well he knew each wandering star
   That once had decked the azure dome,
Would tremble through the clouds of war,
   And like a Prodigal come home.

He perished ere the angel Peace
   Had rolled war's curtain from the sky;
But he shall live when wrong shall cease, —
   The great and good can never die;
For, though his heart lies cold and still,
   We feel its beatings warm and grand,
And still his spirit pulses thrill
   Through all the councils of the land.

The flag of strife at length is furled,
   Rebellion drops the gory knife,
The spring of peace glides up the world,
   Its buds are bursting into life:

Beneath the death-clouds, low and dun,
   The serpent shrinks in black despair,
We lift our eyes to freedom's sun,
   And see the eagles hovering there.

Oh, for the hosts that sleep to-day,
   Lulled by the sound of southern waves:
The sun that lit them in the fray
   Now warms the flowers upon their graves, —
Sweet flowers that speak like words of love
   Between the forms of friends and foe:
Perchance their spirits meet above,
   Who crossed their battle blades below.

'Twas not in vain the deluge came,
   And systems crumbled in the gloom;
And not in vain have sword and flame
   Robbed home and heart of life and bloom:
The mourner's cross, the martyr's blood,
   Shall crown the world with holier rights;
And Slavery's storm and Slavery's flood
   Leave Freedom's ark on loftier heights.

THE BEAUTIFUL YEARS OF OUR
LOVE.

I STOOD by that stream where the wild roses grew
In the green bloom of summer when Nature looked
    new,
And I thought of the time that I roamed there with
    you,
  In the beautiful years of our love.
We were poor, but the pearl of affection was ours,
And we loved the glad world with its sunshine and
    showers,
For life was a wayside of fountains and flowers,
  In the beautiful years of our love.

Now far from that valley I wander, and dream
Of the raptures that perished with love's morning
    gleam;
And day is more lonely than night used to seem
  In the beautiful years of our love:
For I miss your affection, the rose, and the stream
That murmured its tune by the moon's mellow
    beam:
Ah! pleasure seemed real, and life a bright dream,
  In the beautiful years of our love.

There are isles in Life's ocean we cannot forget
Till the light of its sun in the billow has set,
And our souls never turn but with longing regret
   To the beautiful years of our love:
For we dreamed of the pleasure, and saw not the
      woe,
Which Time o'er the scenes of the future might
      throw,
And we hoped for the joys that we never should
      know,
   In the beautiful years of our love.

As the exile looks back from the waves of the deep
To the blue-fading hills where his forefathers sleep,
Oh, thus when the waves of the present time sweep
   O'er the beautiful years of our love,
Do our souls from the future look backward through
      tears
To that shore where the splendor of youth disap-
      pears,
And weep o'er the graves of those time-buried years,
   The beautiful years of our love.

ON THE BEACH.

O Imogene, loved Imogene !
  I stand upon the beach to-day,
And watch the white sails fading dim
O'er the blue deeps that lie serene
  Against the low sky far away,
And wonder if you think of him
Who vainly waits for tide and gale
  To bring his treasures from the main,
Whose hopes went forth like ships that sail,
  And come not back to port again.

A FRAGMENT.

Oh, keels that cleft the seas of long ago!
   Oh, sails that drifted in the morning light,
Till, lost behind the line of ice and snow,
   They gleamed no more upon our longing sight!
What golden waters now around them roll,
   Where isles of beauty sleep in living bloom?
What glories draw them to the Eternal Pole,
   Whose headlands glimmer through the north night
      gloom?

LUTHER OF PIETY HILL.

LUTHER lived among maples on "Piety Hill,"
If out of perdition, he's living there still;
His body is lengthy and lanky and lean,
His virtues are leaner and far between;
His soul — if he has one — is narrow and mean;
If he has a good impulse, it seldom is seen,
For wilfulness covers it up like a screen.
  Oh, the sanctified sinner of "Piety Hill!"

Like the surly Missouri, all muddy and wild,
The stream of his being forever is "riled;"
Abounding in sunken and dangerous snags,
He storms and he sputters, he "jaws" and he nags;
His tongue like the tail of a terrier wags,
Though the tail only waggles when doggie is glad,
While the tongue wags the loudest when Luther is
      mad.
  Oh, the dismal old deacon of "Piety Hill!"

I wonder sometimes what his "new name" will be.
It is hard to find names for such compounds as he.

If his heart were more mellow, he might be called
      hog,
Though he acts like a vulture, and sings like a frog
That croaks at the moon from the brink of a bog;
And he prays like a 'possum, yet inwardly swears, —
His professions are false as the wig that he wears.
    Oh, the pious old pirate of " Piety Hill ! "

In the cycles long past — so the oracles say —
An angel determined to have his own way,
And the effort developed, — oh, shocking to tell ! —
A tail he has worn since the day that he fell
Like a fiery comet from Heaven to hell,
And it follows him yet through the darkness of sin,
A token of rage that was burning within
    When he tried to be ruler on " Piety Hill."

Now, the moral adorning the barb of this "tail"
Is, that charity liveth though prophecies fail:
Let Luther discern from poor Lucifer's fate
That love lifts the latch of the Beautiful Gate;
The pathway to woe leads through malice and hate;
That we carry the signs of the discord we make,
Though we "pay for the Gospel," and pray for
      " Christ's sake,"
    And live among maples on " Piety Hill."

A WESTERN TARN.

Lo ! the Queen of midnight moveth
Where the tacturn lake-fowl looneth,
  Where the Frenchman's dinner jumps,
  Where the Frenchman's diet humps,
  And the owlet whoops and dumps ;
Where the ancient teal carooneth,
And the bashful duckie spooneth
  Round the "tarn "-al "thunder pumps ; "
Where the ultimated polly-
  Wog, resigning "tad " and "pole,"
Leaps a wayward, frisky, jolly
  Frog that whistles at control,
Hops and croaks at polly's folly,
  Fog and slough and marish hole,
Laughs "kerchung " at polly's folly, —
  Bogulated in that hole,
  Prisoned in that pokey hole.

ODE ON A CRACKED BELL.

HEAR the parish chapel bell,
Fractured bell, hear it swell,
Like a drunken Indian's yell;
How the frantic demon rings,
With a crazy wheezy jangle,
Ending in a triple tangle,
Breaking in on song and prayer,
Almost moving saints to swear.
  " *Hang* the bell,
   Whang the bell,
   Bang the bell,
   Dang the bell.
Blast the bell, bell, bell! "
   How it swings,
   How it clings
To the ever-shrieking belfry;
How it jingle, wrangle, dings,
And, like souls in torment, sings
Of unutterable things !
How long, O Lord, how long
Must that phantom of a gong,
Of a heathen Chinese gong,

Wheeze and bray, night and day,
And to meek dissenters say,
When they try to sing or pray,
   " Apostolical succession,
   Apostolical succession,"
With diabolical obsession,
And with infamous expression,
And a damnable transgression
Of all feeling, sense, and sound?

THE EAST AND THE WEST.

Land where the bright day dies
  On the empire's rugged breast,
Where the river sources rise,
  And roll to the east and west,
We hail thee, we hail thee,
  From our high and massive walls,
Where the mighty soul of commerce
  To the "star of empire" calls,
We hail thee, we hail thee
  From many a tender shrine
Where our loving mothers slumber
  In the shade of oak and pine, —
From many a field of battle
  By the blood of heroes blest,
Where the eagles fought together
  For the grand old parent nest.

Land of the morning light,
  Of the pine and drifting snow,
Of the dark green mountain height,
  And rivers that dawnward flow.
We hail thee, we hail thee,
  From our prairies broad and free,

Where the fields of grain are waving
  Like the billows of the sea.
We hail thee, we hail thee,
  From our western summits bold
Where the rocks are tied together
  With yellow threads of gold, —
Where the awful shadows linger
  In our canyons wild and grim,
And the torrent god is singing
  His everlasting hymn.

TO MY MOTHER'S SPIRIT.

Come to my weary heart, wand'ring from duty,
    Spirit that guarded my pathway in youth, —
Come in the beams of thy glorified beauty,
    Smile on a soul that is struggling for truth ;
Thou hast been with me when pleasures were fleeing,
    Silv'ring the nighttime of sorrow with love,
Floating like light through the clouds of my being, —
    Come to me now from thy dwelling above.

Come to my couch when the wide world reposes,
    Watch o'er the slumbers and visions of night,
Rest on my hopes like the dew on the roses ;
    Bring all the budding ones forth to the light.
True as the stars o'er the mountain storm playing,
    Faithful through trial, temptation, and pain,
Thou hast been true when my spirit was straying.
    Come, and I never will grieve thee again.

DAWN.

O Venus! lift your face once more
   Above the surging of the main.
I stand upon a troubled shore
   And look and long for you in vain;
I hear the ocean sob and call,
   Like some great life by love unblest;
I see the waters rise and fall
   Like warring passions in the breast;
The foreheads of the far-off isles
   Are bathing in the springs of dawn:
O Venus! lift your face in smiles,
   And tell me that the night is gone.

THE WOMAN AND THE ANGEL.

SHE sat on the side of the mountain,
  The cataract thundered below;
Above her the roofs of the ages
  Were lifting their thatches of snow;
The landscape was swimming in glory,
  The sky and the earth were in love,
And the great peaks seemed hanging like anchors
  Cast out from the planets above.

'Twas the land where the pale lips of winter
  To the ripe lips of August are pressed;
Where the dead, frozen heart of the rain-drop
  Revives on the lily's white breast;
The cool tide of summer poured round us,
  The bird in the aspen sang sweet,
And the cedar-ribbed shaft of the miner
  Yawned darkly and deep at our feet.

She had turned from the vision of splendor,
  Which Nature before us had spread,
To a form that went down and ascended
  By the windlass that wound overhead;

Then her face, for a moment averted,
  Was raised to the blue of the skies,
And I saw the white soul of the woman
  Shine out through the blue of her eyes.

Unmoved by the voices without her,
  She hearkened to voices within,
And I know that the angels had spoken
  To save her from anguish and sin.
Two spirits contended above her, —
  One fierce and malignant, one mild;
One strove for a treacherous lover,
  One plead for a passion-swayed child.

Then she stooped, as our voices grew louder
  In converse, in music and mirth,
And traced, with her delicate finger,
  Strange lines in the dust of the earth;
She knew not their language or import:
  A spirit directed her hand,
And Heaven alone might interpret
  Those characters written in sand.

She ceased, for the conflict was over,
  The glory had gone from her face;
And a look, half despairing, half loving,
  Came forth, and was throned in its place;
And a storm, broken loose from the mountain,
  Swept over the vale in its flight;
And the sweet bird that sang in the aspen
  Fluttered downward in dumbness and fright.

She descended that night to the valley,
  Oppressed with confusion and pain;
The tempter had conquered the tempted,
  The angel had pleaded in vain:
And the will of her captor surged 'round her
  Like the tide that encircles the bark,
Which, rudderless, crewless, and helpless,
  Drifts out in the desolate dark.

But the angel will follow her footsteps
  O'er mountains, in cities and ships:
She will hear its low call in the midnight,
  And awake to the touch of its lips;
And her soul from the spell shall be lifted,
  For the woman illumines it still;
And the spirit that conquered the tempest
  Shall strengthen the links of her will.

THE INFINITE MOTHER.

I AM mother of Life, and companion of God,
I move in each mote from the suns to the sod,
I brood in all darkness, I gleam in all light,
I fathom all depth and I crown every height;
Within me the globes of the universe roll,
And through me all matter takes impress and soul.
Without me all forms into chaos would fall,
I was under, within and around, over all,
Ere the stars of the morning in harmony sung,
Or the systems and suns from their grand arches
     swung.

I loved you, O Earth, in those cycles profound,
When darkness unbroken encircled you round,
And the fruit of creation, the race of mankind,
Was only a dream in the Infinite mind;
I nursed you, O Earth, ere your oceans were born,
Or your mountains rejoiced in the gladness of morn,
When naked and helpless you came from the womb,
Ere the seasons had decked you with verdure and
     bloom,
And all that appeared of your form or your face
Was a bare, lurid ball in the vast wilds of space.

When your bosom was shaken and rent with alarms
I calmed and caressed you to sleep in my arms,
I sung o'er your pillow the song of the spheres
Till the hum of its melody softened your fears,
And the hot flames of passion burned low in your
    breast
As you lay on my heart like a maiden at rest;
When fevered, I cooled you with mist and with
    shower,
And kissed you with cloudlet and rainbow and
    flower
Till you woke in the heavens arrayed like a queen,
In garments of purple, of gold and of green,
From fabrics of glory my fingers had spun
For the mother of nations and bride of the sun.

There was love in your face, and your bosom rose
    fair,
And the scent of your lilies made fragrant the air,
And your blush in the glance of your lover was
    rare
As you waltzed in the light of his warm yellow
    hair,
Or lay in the haze of his tropical noons,
Or slept 'neath the gaze of the passionless moons, —
And I stretched out my arms from the awful un-
    known
Whose channels are swept by my rivers alone,
And held you secure in your young mother-days,
And sung to your offspring their lullaby lays,

While races and nations came forth from your
    breast,
Lived, struggled, and died, and returned there to
    rest.

All creatures conceived at the Fountain of Cause
Are born of my travail, controlled by my laws;
I throb in their veins and I breathe in their breath,
Combine them for effort, disperse them in death;
No form is too great or minute for my care,
No place so remote but my presence is there.
I bend in the grasses that whisper of spring,
I lean o'er the spaces to hear the stars sing,
I laugh with the infant, I roar with the sea,
I roll in the thunder, I hum with the bee;
From the centre of suns to the flowers of the sod
I am shuttle and loom in the purpose of God,
The ladder of action all spirit must climb
To the clear heights of Love from the lowlands of
    Time.

'Tis mine to protect you, fair bride of the sun,
Till the task of the bride and the bridegroom is
    done;
Till the roses that crown you shall wither away,
And the bloom on your beautiful cheek shall decay;
Till the soft golden locks of your lover turn gray
And palsy shall fall on the pulses of Day;
Till you cease to give birth to the children of men,
And your forms are absorbed in my currents
    again, —

But your sons and your daughters, unconquered by
    strife,
Shall rise on my pinions and bathe in my life,
While the fierce glowing splendors of suns cease to
    burn,
And bright constellations to vapor return,
And new ones that rise from the graves of the old,
Shine, fade, and dissolve like a tale that is told.